The Three Little Pigs

retold by Diane Stortz

Fairy Tale Classics

LANDOLL
Ashland, Ohio 44805

nce there was a mother pig who sent her three little pigs out into the world to seek their fortunes.

"Now remember, boys," she said. "The first thing each of you must do is build a house to keep yourself safe and warm."

Down the road went the first little pig. He met a man with some straw and asked the man to give him a bundle. Then he built himself a little house of straw.

Down the road went the second little pig. He met a man with some sticks and asked the man to give him a load. Then he built himself a little house of sticks.

The third little pig went on down the road until he met a man with some bricks.

"Bricks make a safe, warm house," said the pig. He asked the man to give him a load. Then he built himself a little house of bricks.

A big, bad wolf had heard the news that three little pigs had gone out into the world to seek their fortunes. The wolf was hungry. "I'd like to seek my fortune, too," said the wolf. "And a pig for supper is a fine place to start."

First, the wolf knocked on the door of the little straw house and said, "Little pig, little pig, let me come in."

"Not by the hair of my chinny chin chin," said the pig.

"Then I'll huff and I'll puff and I'll blow your house in," said the wolf. And he huffed, and he puffed, and he blew down the little straw house. But the first little pig ran to safety inside the house of sticks built by his brother.

Soon the wolf knocked on the door of the little stick house, and said, "Little pig, little pig, let me come in."

"Not by the hair of my chinny chin chin," said the second little pig.

"Then I'll huff and I'll puff and I'll blow your house in," said the wolf. And he huffed, and he puffed, and he blew down the little stick house. This time both little pigs ran to safety inside the house of bricks built by their brother.

Soon the wolf knocked at the door of the little brick house and said, "Little pig, little pig, let me come in."

"Not by the hair of my chinny chin chin," said the third little pig.

"Then I'll huff and I'll puff and I'll blow your house in," said the wolf. So he huffed, and he puffed, but he could not blow the house down.

The wolf could see that all this huffing and puffing was not going to get him a pig for supper.

"Little pig," called the wolf. "Do you like turnips?"

"Oh, yes," said the first little pig.

"Then go with me tomorrow to Farmer Smith's turnip field. I will call for you at six o'clock."

"All right," the first little pig said sweetly. But he got up at five, went to the turnip field by himself, and carried home plenty of turnips. He was safely inside his house with his brothers when the wolf came at six o'clock.

Τhe wolf was angry but he tried not to show it. "Little pig," he called. "Do you like apples?"

"Oh, yes," said the second little pig.

"Then come with me tomorrow to the apple orchard on the hill. I will call for you at five o'clock."

"All right," the second little pig said sweetly. But he got up at four o'clock, went to the apple orchard by himself, and carried home plenty of apples. He was busy baking an apple pie when the wolf arrived at five.

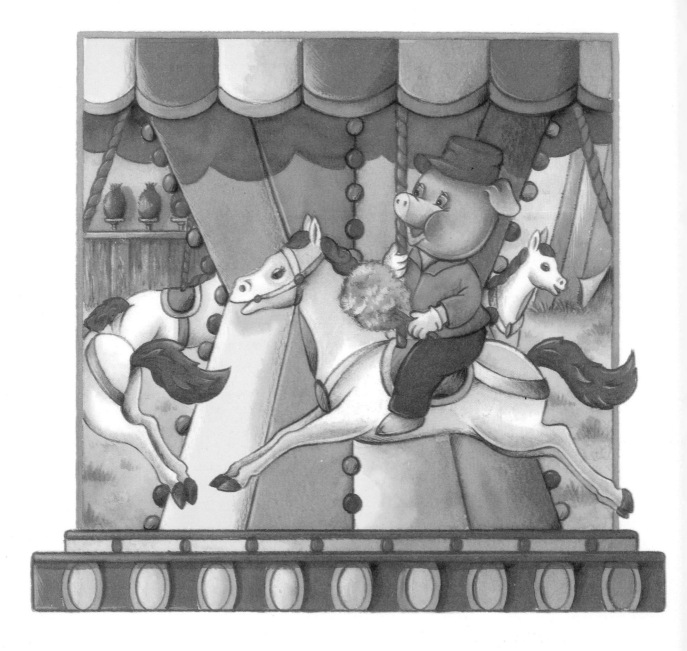

he wolf was angry but he tried not to show it.

"Little pig," he called. "Do you like fairs?"

"Oh yes," said the third little pig. "I love to go to fairs."

"Then go to the country fair with me. I shall call for you tomorrow at three o'clock."

"All right," the third little pig said sweetly. But he got up early and went to the fair by himself. He played the games, ate cotton candy, and bought a barrel to hold rainwater.

He was rolling the barrel toward home when he saw the wolf coming. When he jumped inside the barrel to hide, it began to roll straight at the wolf. The wolf was terrified by the loud, rolling barrel and he turned and ran straight for home.

The wolf was running out of patience and ideas. He climbed up on the roof of the little brick house.

When the wolf felt the heat rising up through the chimney, he decided to have cornmeal mush for supper instead of pig. So he went away, and that was the end of the big, bad wolf...but not the end of the story. The three little pigs lived a long and happy life in the little brick house, where they were always safe and warm. (Thanks for the good advice, Mom!)